Debbie G. Harman
2003

The Book of Mormon Says . . .

Book of Mormon stories that my parents read to me . . .

are about . . .

The
Book of
Mormon
Says . . .

Illustrations by
Debbie G. Harman

The Book of Mormon says . . .
The gospel makes us happy.

Lehi says—
I beheld a tree, whose fruit was desirable to make one happy . . . wherefore, I began to be desirous that my family should partake of it also.

1 Nephi 8:10,12

Knowest thou the meaning of the tree which thy Father saw? Yea, it is the love of God, which sheddeth

I am a Child of God

AND IT IS the GREATEST

OF ALL THE GIFTS of God♥

and which is white above all that is white yea and pure above all that is pure and ye shall feast upon that fruit even until ye are filled, that ye hunger not, neither shall ye thirst. Alma 32:42

which is sweet above that which is sweet, and which is precious, which is most precious,

And the Angel said unto me Behold the Lamb of God...

HOLD TO THE ROD...THE IRON ROD... IS THE WORD OF GOD 'TWILL SAFELY GUIDE US THROUGH

And because of... your diligence... and faith and your patience with the word in nourishing it, that it may take hold in you, behold by and by ye shall pluck the fruit thereof,

itself abroad in the hearts of the children of men; wherefore it is the most desirable above all things,

Yea and most joyous to the soul.

1 Nephi 11: 21-22

The Book of Mormon
says . . . Be obedient.

Nephi says—
. . . I will go and do the
things which the Lord
hath commanded, for I
know that the Lord
giveth no command-
ments unto the children
of men, save he shall
prepare a way for them
that they may accom-
plish the thing which he
commandeth them.

1 Nephi 3:7

The Book of Mormon says
. . . Always say your prayers.

Enos says—
And my soul hungered; and I
kneeled down before my
Maker, and I cried unto him in
mighty prayer and supplica-
tion for mine own soul; and all
the day long did I cry unto him;
yea, and when the night
came I did still raise
my voice high . . .

Enos 1:4

All over the world at the end of day...

Heavenly Father's children kneel down to pray

The Book of Mormon says . . .
Show kindness to others.

King Benjamin says—
I would that ye should impart of your substance to the poor, every man according to that which he hath, such as feeding the hungry, clothing the naked, visiting the sick and administering to their relief, both spiritually and temporally, according to their wants.

Mosiah 4:26

The Book of Mormon says . . .
I can gain a testimony.

Alma says—
Know ye not that I speak the truth? Yea, ye know that I
speak the truth; and you ought to tremble before God.

Mosiah 12:30

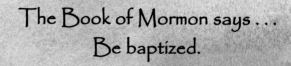

The Book of Mormon says . . .
Be baptized.

Alma says—

. . . and now, as ye are desirous to come into the fold of God, and to be called his people . . . if this be the desire of your hearts, what have you against being baptized in the name of the Lord, as a witness before him that ye have entered into a covenant with him, that ye will serve him and keep his commandments . . . ?

Mosiah 18:8–10

My Baptismal Covenant

I Promise	Heavenly Father Promises
To take upon me the name of Jesus Christ and stand as a witness of Him at all times and in all things and in all places	To forgive me when I repent
To always remember Jesus and love and help others like He would.	To give me the gift of the Holy Ghost
To keep His commandments	To let me live with Heavenly Father and Jesus FOREVER

The Book of Mormon says . . .
We can share the gospel with others.

Ammon says—
. . . I am called by his Holy Spirit to teach these things unto this people, that they may be brought to a knowledge of that which is just and true.

Alma 18:34

What man of you, having an hundred sheep, if he lose one of them, doth not leave the ninety

The Book of Mormon says . . .
I can repent.

The Anti-Nephi-Lehies say—
Oh, how merciful is our God! And now behold, since it has been as much as we could do to get our stains taken away from us, and our swords are made bright, let us hide them away that they may be kept bright, as a testimony to our God at the last day . . .

Alma 24:15

Therefore, whoso Repenteth and cometh unto . . . Me As a little CHILD him will I Receive . . .

I want my life to be as clean as earth right after rain.

therefore Repent and Come unto Me

3 Nephi 9:22

Now, if ye give place, that a seed may be... ...nted in your heart... ...Yea it will strengthen your FAITH

The Book of Mormon says . . .
Have faith.

Alma says—
. . . faith is not to have a perfect knowledge of things; therefore if ye have faith ye hope for things which are not seen, which are true.

Alma 32:21

or ye will say I know that this is a good seed . . . for behold it sprouteth and beginneth to grow. ALMA 32: 28-30

In Memory of our God, our religion, and freedom, and our peace, our wives and our children.

The Book of Mormon says . . . Stand up for what is right.

Moroni says—
Behold, whosoever will maintain this title upon the land, let them come forth in the strength of the Lord . . .

"In memory of our God, our religion, and freedom, and our peace, our wives, and our children."

Alma 46:12, 20

The Book of Mormon says . . .
Be brave and trust in God.

Helaman says—
And now I say unto you my . . .
brother Moroni, that never had I
seen so great courage, nay, not amongst
all the Nephites . . . they had been taught
by their mothers, that if they did not
doubt, God would deliver them.

Alma 56:45–47

Take upon you my whole armor, that ye may be able to withstand the evil day... The breastplate of righteousness...

The Book of Mormon says . . .
Jesus is our Savior

Samuel the Lamanite says—
. . . then cometh the Son of God to redeem all
those who shall believe on his name . . . and behold,
there shall a new star arise, such an one as ye never
have beheld; and this also shall be a sign unto you.

Helaman 14:2–5

For unto you is born this day
in the city of David a Saviour,
which is Christ the Lord.
And this shall be a sign unto you;
Ye shall find the babe
wrapped in swaddling clothes,
lying in a manger.

Luke 2:11,12

The Book of Mormon says . . .
Be a good example.

Jesus says—
And behold, I am the light and the life of the world.

3 Nephi 11:11

The Book of Mormon says . . .
Families are forever.

Jesus says—
And he shall turn the heart of the fathers to the children,
and the heart of the children to the fathers . . .

3 Nephi 25:6

But ye will teach them to walk in the ways of truth and soberness; ye will teach them to love one another, and to serve one another.

Mosiah 4:15

Families are Forever

The Book of Mormon says . . .
Jesus is the Son of God.

Mormon says—
Now these things are written . . . that they may be persuaded that Jesus is the Christ, the Son of the living God . . .

Mormon 5:12–14

And when ye shall receive these things, I would exhort you that ye would ask God, the Eternal Father, in the name of Christ, if these things are not true; and if ye will ask with a sincere heart . . . having faith in Christ, he will manifest the truth of it unto you, by the power of the Holy Ghost.

Moroni 10:4